C000179676

DISCOVER HIDDEN WORLDS

BUGS

By Heather Amery and Jane Songi

A GOLDEN BOOK · NEW YORK

Western Publishing Company, Inc., Racine, Wisconsin 53404

Printed in Italy

© 1994 Reed International Books Limited. All rights
reserved. First published in Great Britain in 1993
by Hamlyn Children's Books, an imprint of Reed
Children's Books Limited, Michelin House, 81 Fulham
Road, London SW3 6RB, England. No part of this book
may be reproduced or copied in any form without
written permission from the publisher. All trademarks
are the property of Western Publishing Company, Inc.
Library of Congress Catalog Card Number: 93-73529
ISBN: 0-307-15664-8/ISBN: 0-307-65664-0 (lib. bdg.)
A MCMXCIV
Printed and bound in Italy by L.E.G.O. s.p.a.

CONTENTS

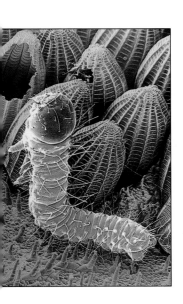

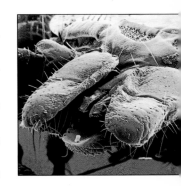

INTRODUCTION

Look closely at the world around you. All sorts of small things you might never have noticed before—a grain of sugar, a tiny insect, a speck of dust—may come into view. And if you use a magnifying glass, you will surely see even more.

Microscopes that use light and have several glass magnifying lenses were invented nearly 400 years ago. For the first time, scientists could see the germs that cause disease, the countless cells in our blood, and millions of other things that no one knew existed. Modern light-using microscopes can magnify an object up to 1,000 times its normal size.

We can look even more closely at the world with electron microscopes, which were invented about 60 years ago. Instead of using light, electron microscopes use a beam of electrons to "look" at tiny things, magnifying them up to 200,000 times.

In this book you will see many bugs—and their body parts—greatly magnified. From caterpillar feet to a fly's eye, the tiniest parts of these small creatures are brought into vivid focus. Color has been added to enhance some of the items shown.

Magnifications in this book are generally given beneath the pictures and consist of a multiplication sign followed by a number. For example, x 25 means that the object is shown at 25 times its actual size. Where there is no magnification given, the photo is simply an enlargement.

▲ The researcher above is using an electron microscope to examine a tiny object. The magnified pictures show up on a television screen.

▼ The technician below is using a light microscope to study samples of bacteria.

▼ Look closely at a spoonful of sugar, and you can see that each grain is a roughly shaped crystal.

▶ Sugar as it is usually seen.

◀ Magnified 25 times (x 25), sugar resembles a collection of diamonds.

◀ At 50 times their normal size, these sugar crystals look like boulders.

◀ Here is the corner of a sugar crystal magnified 500 times.

5

ANIMALS IN ARMOR

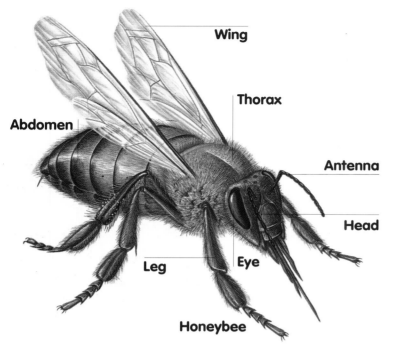

Wing

Thorax

Abdomen

Antenna

Head

Leg

Eye

Honeybee

Insects do not have bones to support their bodies. Instead they are covered with tough, hard skin, like a close-fitting suit of armor. This hard skin gives the insect a shape and protects the soft parts inside, such as the stomach and brain. An insect's body has three main parts—the head, the thorax (middle section), and the abdomen. Mouthparts, eyes, and often antennae are found on the head section. The insect's six legs, and its wings if it has any, are joined to the thorax.

◄ An insect has no nose. It takes the air into its breathing tubes through its spiracles, which are small holes along its thorax and abdomen.

Spiracle of dung fly (x 370)

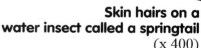

► **Bristling all over.** Insect skin may look smooth, but it is usually covered with hairs, spines, or scales. Just below the surface of the skin are many special nerves. Some of these respond to sound or taste rather than to touch. Flies can actually taste food with their feet.

Skin hairs on a water insect called a springtail (x 400)

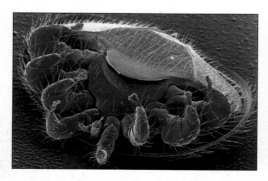

Underside of bee mite (x 75)

Top shell of bee mite (x 75)

◄ Bee mites are tiny creatures that live on bees without harming them. Although their bodies are protected by tough armor plating, mites are not true insects. They are arachnids, the same group of animals that includes spiders.

Fleabitten

Many small insects and other creatures live on animal fur or feathers. Strangely enough, some of these have even smaller creatures living on their bodies. The picture on the right shows the back of a flea that makes its home among the prickles on a hedgehog. Tucked under its scales are several tiny mites that feed on the flea!

Flea mites (x 66)

Hair and spines on springtail skin (x 800)

▼ **Sidesplitting.** Adult insects have a hard outside skin that cannot expand. So to grow bigger, the insect molts. That is, it sheds its old skin and grows a new, larger one. Cicadas, which look like large grasshoppers, may molt up to 30 times during their adult lives.

The greengrocer cicada below lives in Australia. It has come out of its burrow and clambered up a tree trunk to shed its old brown skin. At first its soft new skin is pale green. At this stage it is in great danger of being eaten by birds. Soon its skin will turn hard and dark and be unpleasant to eat.

Greengrocer cicada

▶ After the greengrocer cicada sheds its old brown skin, the crumpled wings on its back open up, enabling it to fly.

NEARLY A MILLION DIFFERENT TYPES OF INSECTS HAVE BEEN IDENTIFIED, BUT THERE MAY BE SEVERAL MILLION MORE TO BE DISCOVERED.

FANTASTIC FLIERS

Swallowtail butterfly

Long before there were birds, there were flying insects. These first appeared about 400 million years ago, even before the dinosaurs. At that time insect wings were simple flaps. Flying allowed insects to migrate to new areas, find new sources of food, and escape from their enemies. As insects developed, most kinds had two pairs of wings. Later, in some species, the two wings on each side joined together. Most flies now have only one pair of wings.

(x 66)

▲ **Shock value.** Some insects, such as butterflies, have beautiful colors and patterns on their wings. These can attract a mate. They can also be a way of scaring off predators. When a butterfly suddenly opens its wings, the large "eye" spots on them may frighten off birds in search of a meal.

A butterfly's wings are covered with tiny colored scales. The scales are actually broad, flat hairs that overlap one another like tiles on a roof.

(x 925)

Scales on butterfly's wing

(x 2,500)

THERE ARE MORE THAN **200,000** KNOWN TYPES OF BUTTERFLIES AND MOTHS.

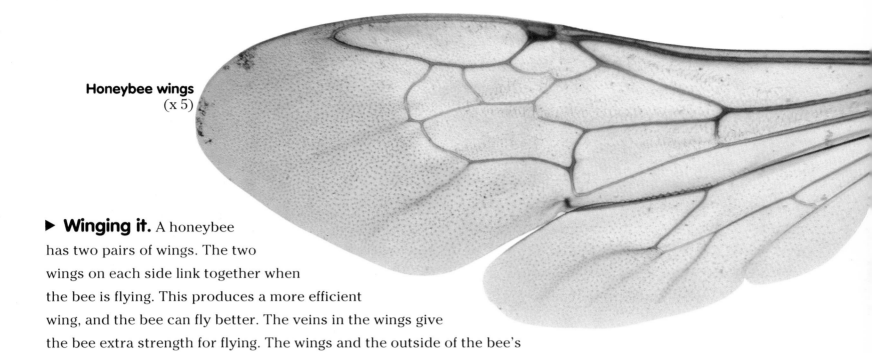

Honeybee wings
(x 5)

▶ **Winging it.** A honeybee
has two pairs of wings. The two
wings on each side link together when
the bee is flying. This produces a more efficient
wing, and the bee can fly better. The veins in the wings give
the bee extra strength for flying. The wings and the outside of the bee's
body are made of the same hard material, called chitin.

   A bee can beat its wings more than 200 times a second and fly at speeds
of up to 7 miles per hour. When resting, a bee folds its wings flat against the
back of its body.

DID YOU KNOW?

*The buzzing noise some
insects make is caused by
their wings beating the air.
The faster they flap their
wings, the higher the pitch
of the sound. A mosquito,
which makes a high-pitched
whine, beats its wings about
600 times a second.*

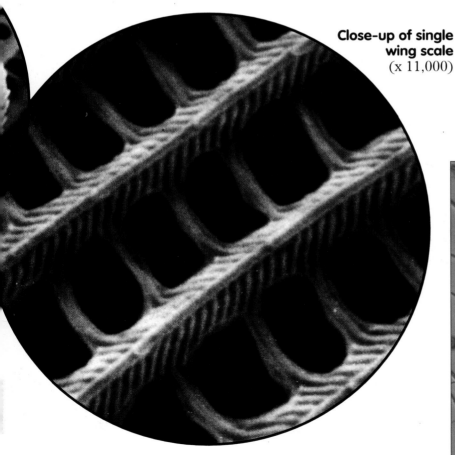

**Close-up of single
wing scale**
(x 11,000)

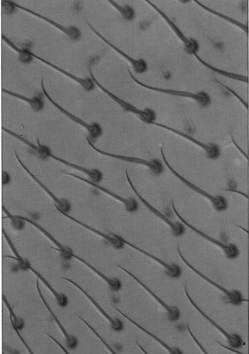

◀ These are the
wing scales of a
cluster fly. Like
most flies, this
insect has only
one pair of true
wings. The
second pair are
just stumps that
help the fly keep
its balance in
the air.

**Cluster fly
wing surface**
(x 1,000)

SUPER SIGHT

Most insects have eyesight good enough to find their way when looking for food and fleeing from danger. Insects have "compound" eyes—eyes that are very complex, with many surfaces, or facets. Some insects have large eyes, with a few hundred facets, while others have enormous eyes, with thousands of facets. All insects can see the colors blue and yellow, but butterflies and a few other insects can also see red.

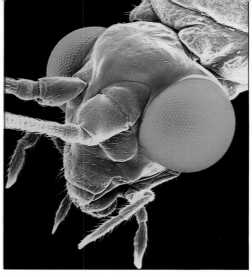

Lacewing
(x 30)

▲ Between the eyes of the lacewing are its antennae, or feelers, each of which is covered with hairs that are very sensitive to touch. The eyes in this photo have been dyed bright orange so they can be seen more clearly.

▼ **Rainbow reflections.** A horsefly has large flat eyes whose bright colors are caused by light reflecting off the many facets. The eyes are made up of hundreds of tiny tightly packed cone-shaped cells, each with a lens at the wide end. These cells are sensitive to light. As light passes through the lens, it is focused onto a light-sensitive "rod." This rod converts the light into electrical signals that are passed on to the insect's brain. The brain then records the pictures the insect sees with its eyes and recognizes the objects as food or as things the insect should avoid.

Whitefly's eye
(x 530)

Horsefly
(x 6)

▶ The eye of a whitefly is made up of 57 light-sensitive cells. Whiteflies produce wax, which protects their bodies. The specks shown are wax on the eye's surface.

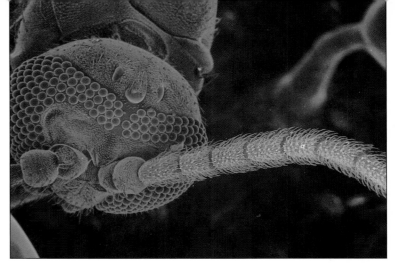

Sciarid fly
(x 130)

DID YOU KNOW?

Insects with compound eyes see the world in many tiny pictures that combine to make up one picture in their brain. This is because each facet of their eyes is at a slightly different angle to the others and collects different information. An insect's eyes are extremely good at detecting movement but do not see objects as clearly as human eyes.

▲ **Feelers, tasters, and smellers.** On the head of the sciarid fly are two long, flexible antennae. The antennae are important sense organs and are very sensitive to touch. They are also sensitive to changes in temperature.

Insects use their antennae mainly to find food. If you watch an insect, you will see its antennae flicking quickly about in the air and lightly touching anything the insect has landed on. The antennae can detect chemicals in the air, which is how the insect smells and tastes things.

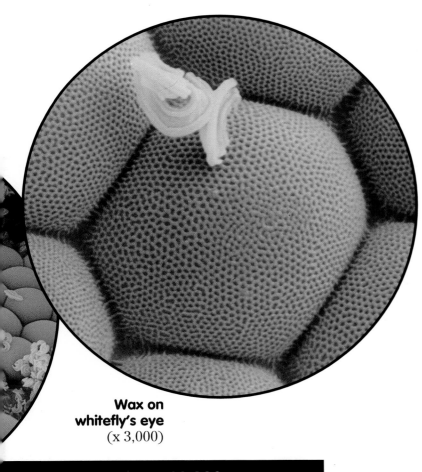

Wax on whitefly's eye
(x 3,000)

A DRAGONFLY HAS **30,000** FACETS IN EACH EYE.

▶ **The large yellow eyes of the tsetse fly bulge out on each side of its head and give the fly a very wide range of vision.**

Tsetse fly
(x 20)

11

FEEDING TIME

Razor edges for slicing, needle-sharp points for piercing, viselike jaws for gripping and chewing—insect mouths come with a wide variety of equipment and in many different shapes and sizes to suit the type of food the insect eats. Insects such as beetles and ants eat wood and seeds. They have strong jawlike structures called mandibles for cutting up their tough food. Butterflies and flies have long mouth tubes to suck up the liquids they feed on.

DID YOU KNOW?

The Malaysian moth, the only known vampire moth, feeds on the blood of buffaloes, tapirs, and other mammals. The moth uses its long, sharp proboscis to drill into a victim's skin and feed on its blood for up to an hour at a time.

▼ **Sweet tooth.** Butterflies feed mainly on flower nectar, the juice of very ripe fruit, and other sweet foods. The sugars in these foods give the butterflies the energy they need to fly. More substantial body-building foods are unnecessary, because butterflies' lives are so short. To eat, butterflies suck up liquids with a long hollow mouth tube, or proboscis.

▼ **A butterfly's proboscis is coiled up under its mouth when it is not in use. Muscles are used to straighten the proboscis before the butterfly feeds.**

Butterfly feeding on flower

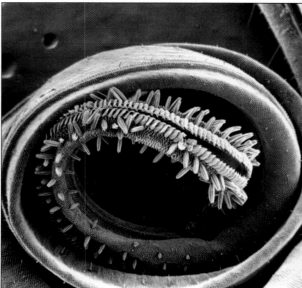

Butterfly's proboscis
(x 25)

12

▼ Sucking up. Blowflies have sucking mouthparts that enable them to feed on dead animals, rotting meat, and animal droppings. As they fly from one source of food to another, they can pick up and carry bacteria on their feet. One type of blowfly is the bluebottle, which will fly into houses in search of food. If food is left uncovered, a bluebottle may land on it and leave disease-causing bacteria behind.

Housefly
(x 35)

Blowfly mouthparts
(x 65)

▲ Houseflies have long trumpet-shaped mouthparts. They suck up liquids from rotting food.

Sweet dreams?

Like tiny vampires, tsetse flies can push their long proboscis through the skin of an animal or a person and suck up blood. These large flies live in tropical Africa and carry parasites that cause serious diseases such as sleeping sickness.

▶ These are the mouthparts of a sheep tick. Sheep ticks are actually wingless flies. Like true ticks, however, they infest a host animal, in this case a sheep.

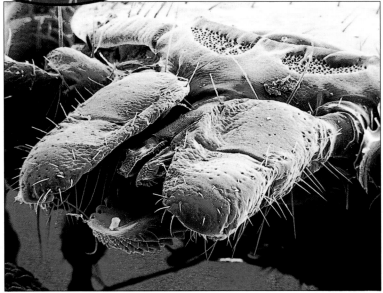

Sheep tick
(x 170)

Tsetse fly
(x 8)

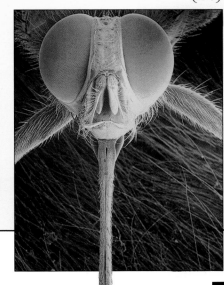

EXTRAORDINARY EGGS

All insects, with a very few exceptions, lay eggs. The eggs have a shell made of chitin, the same material as the hard outside of the insect's body. Many insects lay their eggs where there is a ready supply of food for the newly hatched young. The young insects breaking out of their shells are quite different from their parents. They have to go through several changes before they look like them.

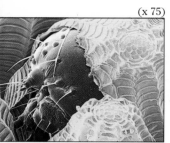

(x 75)

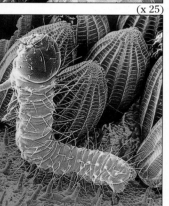

(x 25)

(x 10)

◄ **These large white butterfly caterpillars** *(top)* are beginning to break out of their shells on the underside of a leaf. The eggs are on the leaf only a few days before caterpillars begin to hatch, a process lasting only a few minutes. The caterpillars eat the shells as their first meal and then eat part of the leaf. The bristles on their body help protect them from predators.

Eggs and caterpillars of a large white butterfly

► **Down the tube.** This egg, being laid by a female fruit fly, is coming out of a tube at the end of the fly's body. Many female insects have a point at the end of their egg-laying tube so that they can drill small holes in soft fruit such as cherries or plums. They later lay an egg in each hole, where it will be safe from predators and will not be crushed as the fruit grows. Insects that lay eggs in wood or leaves have egg-laying tubes with straight, sharp ends. These bladelike structures are used to cut slits in the wood or leaf for egg laying.

Fruit fly laying an egg
(x 85)

Moth egg
(x 110)

ONLY THE QUEEN HONEYBEE LAYS EGGS. SHE MAY LAY UP TO 600,000 EGGS IN THREE TO FIVE YEARS.

Big families!

Houseflies lay their eggs in batches of up to 150 at a time. One female may lay as many as 2,000 eggs in her month-long life. The eggs are laid in manure, in trash cans, and on meat. After about 20 hours, maggots hatch out of the eggs. The maggots go through two changes before they become adult flies, about 10 days later.

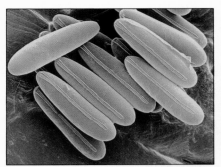

Housefly eggs
(x 9)

DID YOU KNOW?

Human warble flies, which live in North and South America, lay their eggs on the bodies of female mosquitoes or other flies. When the mosquito or fly lands on a person to bite or feed, the eggs hatch. The newborn maggots burrow into the victim's skin, where they feed and grow, eventually causing a boil.

▼ **Egg assortment.** Insect eggs come in all shapes and sizes. Small insects usually lay small eggs, but some aphids lay eggs that are nearly as large as the females themselves. One type of dobsonfly, which can be very large, lays 2,000 to 3,000 eggs in a tiny mass the size of a pea.

Some insect eggs are flat, like scales. Some butterfly eggs are almost round, but others are shaped like cones. Sap-sucking insects called leafhoppers lay long tube-shaped eggs.

The eggshells of some insects are smooth. Others have spines or deep ridges on them to protect them. After laying their eggs, many insects cover them to hide them from predators.

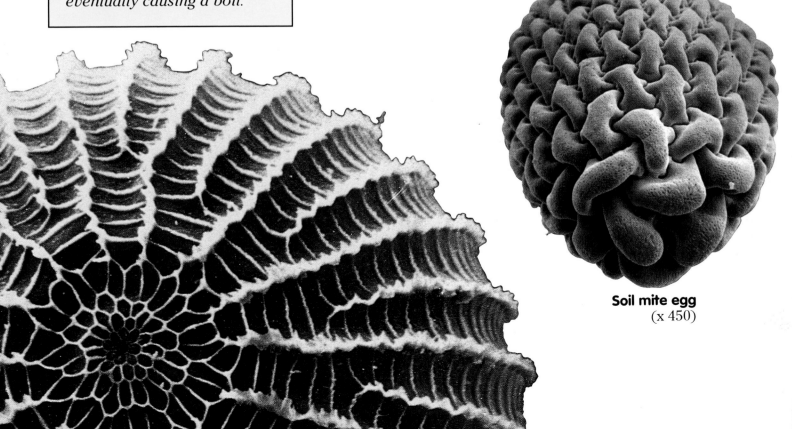

Soil mite egg
(x 450)

LIFE CYCLES

When insects hatch from their eggs, they usually look completely different from their parents. They emerge from the eggs as maggots, caterpillars, or grubs. Most of them make up to four complete changes before they become flies, butterflies, beetles, or other adult insects. Then they are ready to fly, mate, and lay their eggs. During each change, called a metamorphosis, they may live in different places and eat different types of food.

DID YOU KNOW?

Some caterpillars build a chrysalis, or cocoon, around themselves in the autumn and do not come out of it until the spring. There is one type of cicada that stays in its chrysalis for up to 17 years before it emerges as an adult!

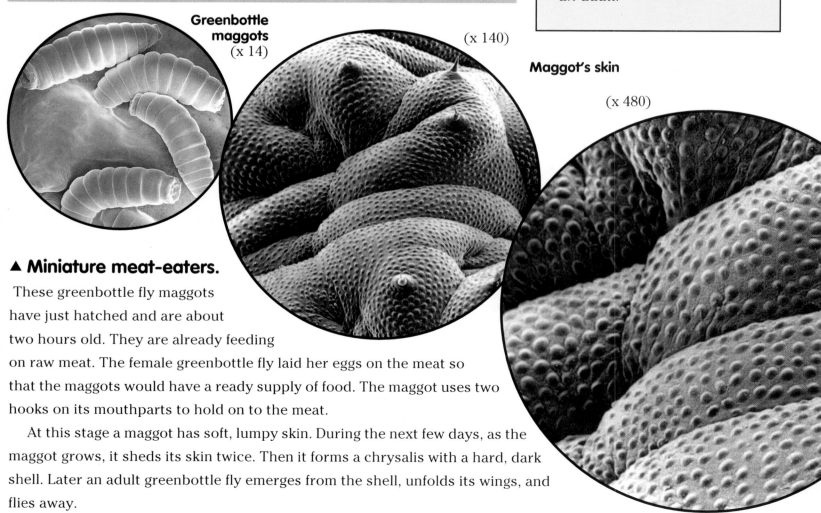

Greenbottle maggots
(x 14)

(x 140)

Maggot's skin

(x 480)

▲ Miniature meat-eaters.

These greenbottle fly maggots have just hatched and are about two hours old. They are already feeding on raw meat. The female greenbottle fly laid her eggs on the meat so that the maggots would have a ready supply of food. The maggot uses two hooks on its mouthparts to hold on to the meat.

At this stage a maggot has soft, lumpy skin. During the next few days, as the maggot grows, it sheds its skin twice. Then it forms a chrysalis with a hard, dark shell. Later an adult greenbottle fly emerges from the shell, unfolds its wings, and flies away.

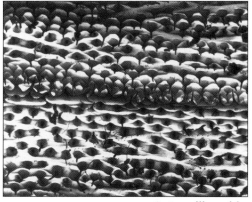

◄ Caterpillars eat an enormous amount of food and grow very quickly, shedding their skin up to four times as they get bigger.

Caterpillar skin
(x 175)

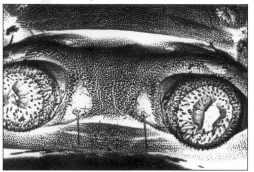

◄ Most types of caterpillars have eight pairs of legs. The feet on the back pair have tiny hooks that enable the caterpillar to grip things tightly.

Caterpillar feet
(x 25)

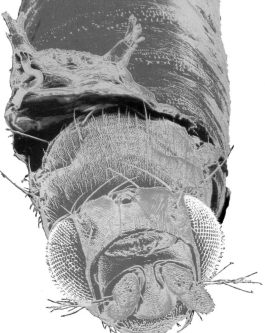

◄ This adult fruit fly is just emerging from its chrysalis. A bag of skin on its head is pumped up with blood, which causes the hard shell to split. The bag then shrinks back into the insect's head.

Fruit fly hatching
(x 60)

▼ **Blossoms for breakfast.** A monarch butterfly caterpillar uses its hooked feet to cling to the stem of a milkweed plant as it feeds on one of the flower petals. While chewing, its strong jaws move from side to side rather than up and down.

Caterpillars have many ways of defending themselves against predators, especially birds. Some caterpillars look just like a leaf or part of a plant stem, while others can quickly drop off a leaf to hide. A few are brilliantly colored or have large bright spots on their heads. These spots look like huge eyes, which scares off birds.

Monarch butterfly caterpillar

▲ These red and green aphids are probing the stem and veins of a rose leaf to locate and then suck out the juice.

SAP SUCKERS

Have you ever been in a garden and seen huge swarms of bugs nearly burying a plant? Tiny aphids are a common sight on the leaves, stems, bark, and roots of many different plants. Usually green, red, brown, or black, aphids are also called plant lice, greenflies, blackflies, or woolly aphids. They suck the sap from plants, causing the leaves to curl up and wither. Eventually the plants wilt and die. Aphids damage fruits and vegetables such as apples, grapes, beans, and cabbages, and they spread plant diseases from one crop to another.

▶ **Population explosion.** The time of year that an aphid is born seems to determine much about its life. Aphids born in the spring are wingless and female. Reproducing rapidly, the aphids crowd themselves onto plants in huge numbers, eventually destroying them. When overpopulation causes food to run out, usually in the fall, aphids produce winged females that fly off in cloudlike swarms to find new supplies.

Aphid
(x 100)

DID YOU KNOW?

Female aphids do not need to mate with males to produce eggs that will hatch. About 50 daughters at a time can be hatched without mating. These young daughters already have eggs developing inside their bodies. Ultimately, aphids can produce as many as 12 generations in a summer.

▶ This aphid is using its mouthpart to feed on a peach tree leaf. The wrinkled surface of the leaf shows that the plant has been invaded by aphids before.

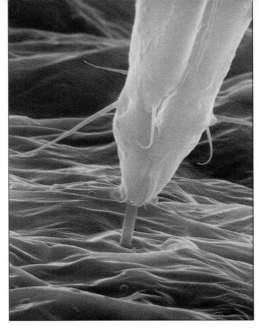

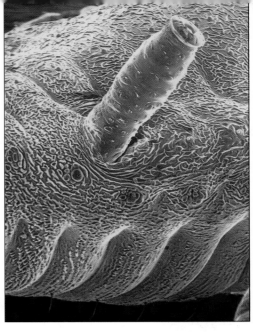

Mouthpart of aphid
(x 550)

Cornicle on aphid's back
(x 250)

Waxy weapons. On the backs of some aphids are two short tube-shaped weapons called cornicles *(above right)*. These are a defense against the aphid's many predators, which include other insects such as ladybugs, hover flies, and lacewings, as well as some small birds. When an aphid is threatened, the cornicles produce a red waxy substance. The wax may make the predator's mouth slippery, allowing the aphid to escape.

Woolly aphids have cornicles that produce fluffy strands of white wax. This is what gives them their name. These aphids live on apple, maple, and alder trees. The row of holes below the cornicle are spiracles, the air holes through which the aphid breathes. Each spiracle can open and close separately.

IN ONE YEAR THE DESCENDANTS OF ONE APHID WOULD WEIGH AS MUCH AS **600** MILLION PEOPLE — IF EVERY DESCENDANT SURVIVED THAT LONG!

LIVING TOGETHER

Ants are found nearly everywhere on earth. In fact, there are about 8,000 different types—most living in hot tropical countries. Ants live together in colonies, the largest of which may have more than 200,000 insects. Each colony has one or more egg-laying females called queens. Other females known as workers look after the queen and her eggs. Male ants are found in the colony only during the mating season each year. There are often two kinds of workers in a colony: ordinary worker ants and soldier ants. Some ants have a stinger for defending themselves, while others squirt an acid from their bodies.

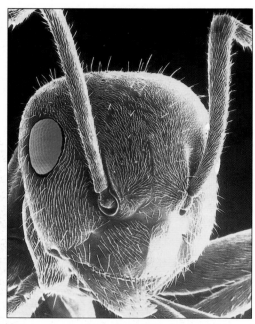

Head of black garden ant
(x 45)

▲ Black garden ants live in nests started by a queen ant. These nests are often found under stones along lawns and paths and even under the walls of houses.

▶ **Slave labor.** These powerful jaws belong to a female black garden ant. Black garden ants feed on small insects such as caterpillars, earwigs, and other ants. Worker ants feed the grubs after they hatch, supplying them with drops of liquid food and breaking hard food into small pieces with their jaws. The newly hatched grubs are kept warm and damp until they change into adults. The worker ants also bring food to the queen ant.

**Jaws of
black garden ant**
(x 75)

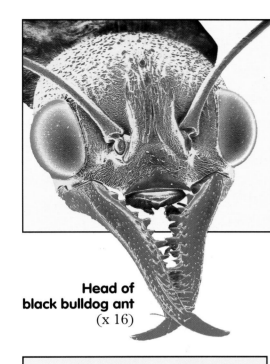

Head of black bulldog ant
(x 16)

Spider hunt

At left is the head of a black bulldog ant, which lives on the coasts of Australia and Tasmania. About as long as an almond, these ants have very painful bites. The adults live on the sweet juices of plants and hunt for insects and spiders to feed their young.

DID YOU KNOW?

Some ants use aphids the way people use cows for milk. The ants stroke the aphids with their antennae, causing the aphids to produce tiny drops of liquid called honeydew, which the ants drink. In return, the ants protect the aphids' eggs from predators.

▶ **Sensitive soles.** Black garden ants have feet that bristle with many sensitive hairs. Each foot also has two large claws on either side for grasping things. Between each pair of claws is a tiny round suction pad. The pad helps the ant climb up walls and tree trunks and even walk upside down on the underside of slippery leaves.

Foot of black garden ant
(x 200)

Swarm of black garden ants

◀ **The largest black garden ants are the queens. The smaller ones are the males. Once they have mated, the queen ants go off to make their nests, and the males soon die.**

BUSY BEES

Not all bees live in crowded hives or nests. Most types live alone. They make nests in hollow trees, holes in the ground, or cracks in rocks. They lay their eggs in the nests, put in a supply of food, and then leave the eggs to hatch on their own. It is the best-known bees, the honeybees, that live in large colonies. All bees feed on the nectar and pollen of flowers and are important to the pollination of plants and trees.

◄ This bee is feeding on a dandelion, probing for nectar with its long dark tongue.

Bumblebee

DID YOU KNOW?

After visiting up to 100 different flowers, honeybees go back to the hive and spit up the nectar they have swallowed. Worker bees mix this substance with their saliva and then store it in combs, where it eventually thickens into what is known as honey. The bees eat this store of food in winter and also use it to feed their young.

► **Pollen by the basket.**
Honeybees collect pollen grains from various flowers to take back to their hives. First, they gather the pollen with their front feet. Special "brushes" on their legs are used to collect pollen that has stuck to their hairy bodies and antennae. The honeybees then pack the pollen into tiny "baskets" made of long hairs on their back legs.

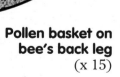

Pollen basket on bee's back leg
(x 15)

WHEN A HONEYBEE FINDS A SOURCE OF NECTAR, IT GOES BACK TO THE HIVE AND DOES A SPECIAL "DANCE" TO TELL THE OTHER BEES WHERE TO FIND IT.

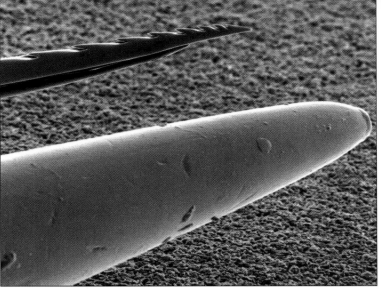

Bee's stinger
(x 16)

Bee's stinger *(top)* **and the point of a needle**
(x 240)

All aboard!

Bee lice live on the bodies of honeybees, usually the queen bees. They ride on the bee's back and obtain food from inside her mouthparts. Bee lice lay their eggs on the honeycomb wax in beehives.

▲ **A sore point.** A few kinds of bees, including honeybees, have stingers. Each female worker bee has a stinger at the end of her body. The stinger is actually the bee's egg-laying tube, which is not needed by the female worker bees for laying eggs. When a bee or her hive is in danger, the female pushes out the stinger and presses it into the intruder. The barb contains a poison that causes a painful wound in people and can paralyze insects.

Bee louse
(x 130)

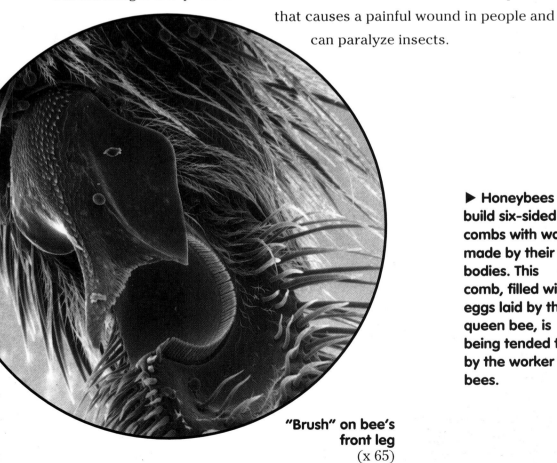

▶ **Honeybees build six-sided combs with wax made by their bodies. This comb, filled with eggs laid by the queen bee, is being tended to by the worker bees.**

"Brush" on bee's front leg
(x 65)

23

FANCY FOOTWORK

There are more than 90,000 different kinds of flies. Flies live almost everywhere, in all sorts of climates. Most, though, breed only in warm places. Flies may lay their eggs in water, under the ground, on plant leaves or stems, in garbage piles, or among animal droppings. They tend to lay their eggs where there is plenty of food for their offspring to eat as they hatch. The young, called maggots, eventually develop chrysalises, from which flying adults emerge.

▶ **Sticky steps.** On each of its six feet, a housefly has two claws with which it clings to rough surfaces. Each foot also has a cushion made of many tiny tubes. Together these tubes act as a suction pad so that the fly can stick to smooth surfaces. A sticky substance that helps the fly to hold on is also released by the tubes. That's how a housefly can walk up walls and even hang upside down on ceilings!

Housefly's leg
(x 80)

Housefly's foot
(x 110)

A HOUSEFLY CAN LAY UP TO **2,000** EGGS IN ITS LIFETIME, WHICH IS ONLY ABOUT FOUR WEEKS LONG.

Sole of housefly's foot
(x 420)

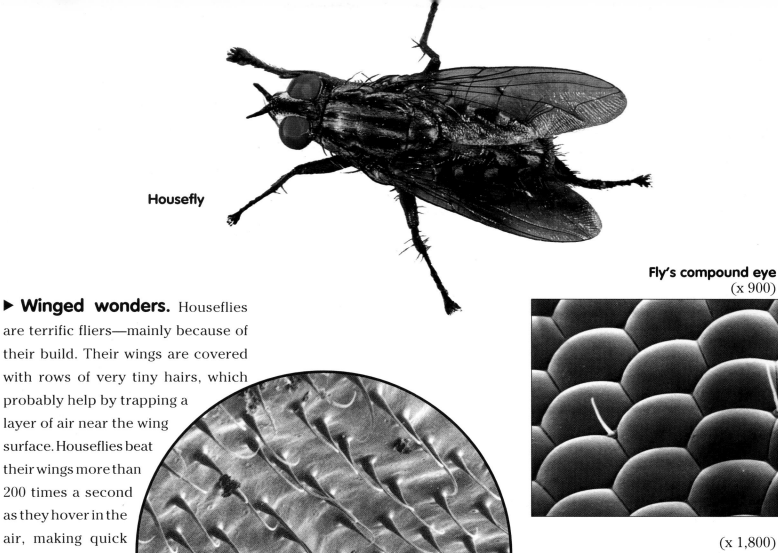

Housefly

Fly's compound eye
(x 900)

▶ **Winged wonders.** Houseflies are terrific fliers—mainly because of their build. Their wings are covered with rows of very tiny hairs, which probably help by trapping a layer of air near the wing surface. Houseflies beat their wings more than 200 times a second as they hover in the air, making quick darting movements and turning upside down.

(x 1,800)

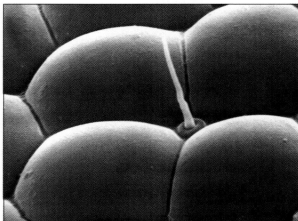

Housefly's wing
(x 340)

DID YOU KNOW?

After a housefly has eaten, it vomits its food and then eats it again. The spots you see on dirty windows where flies have been is this substance. The vomit often carries germs that, if left on food, can spread serious diseases.

▲ Flies can detect the tiniest movement and react very quickly. They do this by using their compound eyes and the many hairs on their bodies, which can sense the slightest air current.

HIGH JUMPERS

Fleas are tiny insects that live on people, birds, and other animals, feasting on their blood. Different kinds of fleas prefer to live on different kinds of animals, but if a flea is really hungry, it will latch on to anything nearby. Fleas that usually live on rabbits will sometimes move on to the cats that hunt the rabbits. Cat and dog fleas will also bite people. Most fleas only cause itchiness, but some can spread serious diseases.

▶ **This cat flea is crawling through the fur at the edge of a cat's ear. Cat fleas can live for a long time without food, but when a cat passes, they quickly jump on for a meal.**

Flea on cat's ear

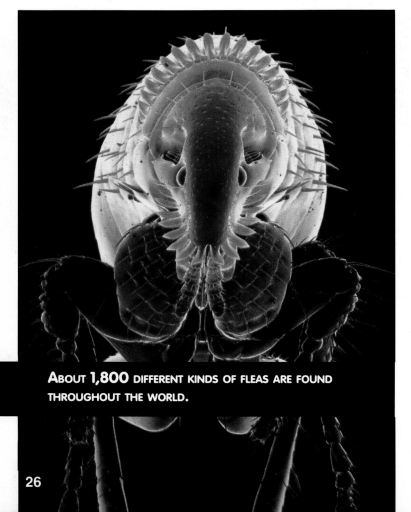

ABOUT **1,800** DIFFERENT KINDS OF FLEAS ARE FOUND THROUGHOUT THE WORLD.

▶ **A body for burrowing.** Like all fleas, cat fleas have no wings. Using its tall, thin body, the flea can move easily through a cat's fur. The spines on its head and abdomen help the flea cling to the fur. The flea uses its mouthparts, or mandibles, to pierce the cat's skin and suck its blood.

Fleas lay tiny white eggs on their hosts. The eggs drop to the ground, where they hatch as maggots. The maggots feed on garbage and animal droppings. They then spin a cocoon, in which they can stay for a long time. Shortly after fleas emerge as adults, they have to find just the right animal to feed on.

Head of cat flea
(x 110)

26

Spiky springer. Fleas are very good at jumping. If a rabbit flea falls off its host, it waits until another rabbit passes by. Then it leaps and spins in the air. Spinning helps it get a good grip when it lands on the rabbit's fur.

Rabbit fleas that live on mother rabbits move to newborn baby rabbits to feed and mate. They lay their eggs in the rabbit's dung, where there is plenty of food for the maggots when they hatch.

Jumping cat flea
(x 25)

▲ A flea uses its long back legs to spring into the air.

Neck of cat flea
(x 1,600)

Body of cat flea
(x 660)

DID YOU KNOW?

Fleas that live on people are the best jumpers of all. They can leap about 130 times their own height. If people could jump as high as this, they would be able to leap over the top of a 70-story building!

Deadly disease

Fleas that live on rats can spread a deadly disease called bubonic plague. In the 14th century about a quarter of all the people in Western Europe died of this disease after being bitten by infected rat fleas.

Rat flea
(x 450)

Meet the Beetles

Beetles are the largest group of animals on earth. About 300,000 different kinds are found in various parts of the world. All beetles have a tough cover on their back formed by their closed top wings. These wings are never used for flying. Instead they fit together to form a protective case over the beetle's true wings. The flying wings fold underneath the top wings when not in use.

Mint leaf beetle

▲ Many beetles are brilliantly colored. They may be easy to see, but birds usually leave them alone because the hard shells of the beetles make them a very tough meal.

▼ **Boring beast.** A weevil is a type of beetle. It has a long head and a long snout with small jaws at the end of it. Many weevils use their snouts to bore into grain, seeds, rice, nuts, and trees. They can destroy huge amounts of stored food as well as some nut-producing trees. Weevils lay their eggs in the grain or nut. When the grubs hatch, they feed hungrily on the food item and spoil what is left with their droppings.

Different views of a weevil's foot

(x 160)

(x 145)

▲ Many beetles have hooks on their feet. They also have hundreds of scales or even velvety bristles. These help the beetle to grip smooth surfaces such as leaves and stems as it scurries around searching for something tasty to eat.

Weevil's head
(x 45)

28

DID YOU KNOW?

Water beetles keep an air supply under their wing cases for underwater diving. They use the air to breathe, but it can also help them stay afloat. They swim with their back legs, paddling them like little oars. Then they dive deep in the water to find tiny animals to eat, coming back to the surface again to take in another supply of air.

▶ The Suriname beetle lives in Suriname, South America. It has long, sensitive antennae that it uses to smell food, find its way back to its burrow, and recognize other beetles.

Suriname beetle
(x 32)

Diverse diets. Many beetles have strong, sharp jaws and a nasty bite. They use their jaws to chew rotting wood, thus clearing forests of dead trees. They also feed on dead animals. Some beetles, such as ladybugs, are very useful because they eat aphids or other insect pests.

Beetles lay eggs in water, tree bark, timber in houses, the ground, and many other places. As soon as their grubs hatch from the eggs, they start to feed. Tiny wood-boring beetles make long tunnels in tree stumps and logs. They grow a fungus in the damp tunnels that supplies the beetles and their grubs with food. The grubs retreat into chrysalises before changing into adult beetles.

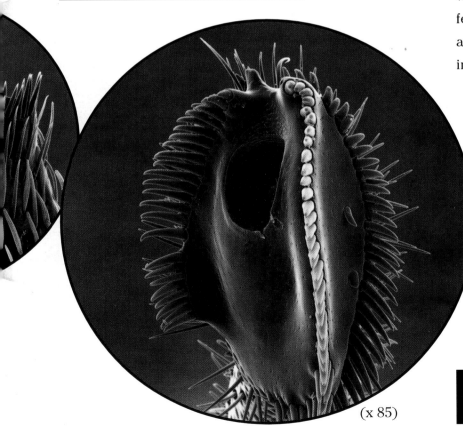

(x 85)

THE GOLIATH BEETLE WEIGHS AS MUCH AS TWO CHICKEN EGGS (ABOUT 4 OUNCES). IT IS ONE OF THE LARGEST FLYING INSECTS.

Head of female mosquito
(x 95)

Vampire Flies

Mosquitoes are best known and most feared for their nasty habit of sucking human blood and for carrying two deadly tropical diseases, malaria and yellow fever. But not all mosquitoes are bloodsuckers and not all of them attack people. Some mosquitoes prefer other mammals and some feed on birds. Among bloodsucking mosquitoes, only the females bite. The males feed on flower nectar and the juice of ripe fruit.

▶ The antennae of this female mosquito may look quite hairy, but those of most male mosquitoes are even bushier. This is one way to tell males and females apart.

Antenna socket of
female mosquito
(x 500)

Jab of germs. When a female mosquito lands on a person, she pushes her long, sharp proboscis through the skin and into the flesh. There are two tubes in the proboscis. A liquid is pumped down the smaller tube. This keeps the blood from clotting. The mosquito sucks up the blood through the other tube. The liquid pumped down may contain tiny disease-carrying parasites that were picked up from the blood of a previously bitten victim. These parasites pass into the bloodstream of the present victim and can cause illness.

EACH YEAR OVER **200** MILLION PEOPLE IN THE TROPICS CONTRACT MALARIA AND **2** MILLION DIE OF IT.

Dancing at dusk

Midges are very small flying insects that like to swarm in dense clouds, or groups, near water, usually on warm evenings. They seem to dance in the air several feet off the ground. Some midges bite, causing an irritating itch. Below is a swarm of South African midges.

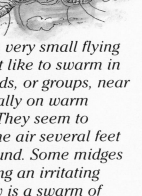

Cloud of midges

▶ Mosquitoes' narrow wings have a fringe of tiny scales. These scales may act like the movable parts of an airplane's wings, helping the insect to fly and maneuver in the air.

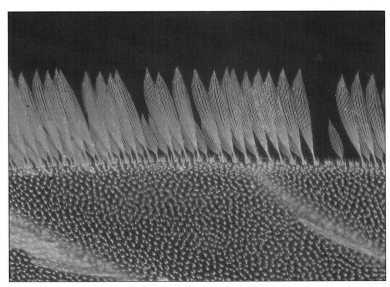

Edge of mosquito's wing
(x 360)

▶ **Balancing trick.** Unlike bees, which have two pairs of wings, mosquitoes have only one functional pair. The second pair look like small drumsticks below the first pair. They help the insect balance when flying.

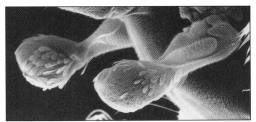

Wing balancers
(x 160)

Some types of mosquitoes fly silently, and their victims become aware of them only when they feel a tiny bite or start to scratch the wound. Other mosquitoes make a high-pitched whining noise. Some mosquitoes fly only during the day, while others are active at night.

▶ Before a female mosquito begins to feed, the hairy tip on her proboscis bends back, exposing the sharp biting and sucking tubes.

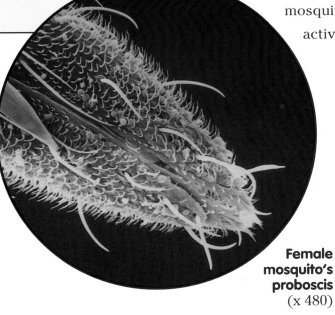

Female mosquito's proboscis
(x 480)

DID YOU KNOW?

The first attempt to build the Panama Canal in Central America was given up after nine years. The main reason was that swarms of disease-carrying mosquitoes often plagued the workers. During that time, nearly 16,000 men working on the canal died from malaria and yellow fever.

Spider's web

▲ A garden spider sits in the center of its web, waiting for an insect to get tangled up in the sticky threads.

WEAVING WIZARDS

Spiders aren't insects. They belong to a group of animals called arachnids. This group also includes scorpions, mites, and ticks. There are more than 30,000 different kinds of spiders found all over the world. Many spiders make webs and other traps to catch their food, but some chase their prey, running fast enough to overtake it. There are also spiders that stalk true insects such as butterflies, jumping on them when the insects are close enough.

(x 24)

Spin cycle. A spider starts its web by spinning a few lines of thin, sticky thread on a bush, in a hedge, or across a ditch. Then it adds more threads from the center to the outside, like the spokes of a wheel. When the spider is finished making its web frame, it walks around it for hours, moving from the middle toward the edge, laying out the cross lines. Finally the spider spins a little platform and waits until an insect such as a fly lands on the sticky mesh or blunders into it.

Spider
(x 40)

SPIDERS SPIN THREAD SO THIN AND LIGHT THAT A PIECE LONG ENOUGH TO GO AROUND THE WORLD WOULD WEIGH ONLY AS MUCH AS AN ORANGE.

◄ The bodies of all spiders are divided into two parts—a head and chest joined together and an abdomen. Spiders have eight legs, two pincer claws, and two jaws.

▼ **Raw silk.** The silken thread that a spider produces comes from tiny tubes called spinnerets at the end of its body. Most spiders have six spinnerets. Each spinneret is a gland with many openings. Very fine threads are drawn out of these openings and join together to make one thread.

Spider webs come in all shapes and sizes. The money spider's web looks like a hammock, with long threads attaching it to a plant. An insect trapped by the threads eventually falls into the hammock, and the spider darts out to gobble it up.

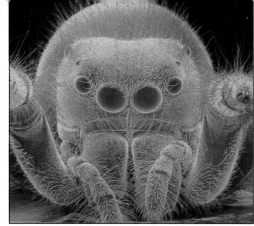

Spider's eyes
(x 12)

▲ **Most spiders have eight eyes. This jumping spider has four large eyes on its face and four more eyes on the top of its head.**

Spider's spinnerets

(x 310)

Spider eating
(x 18)

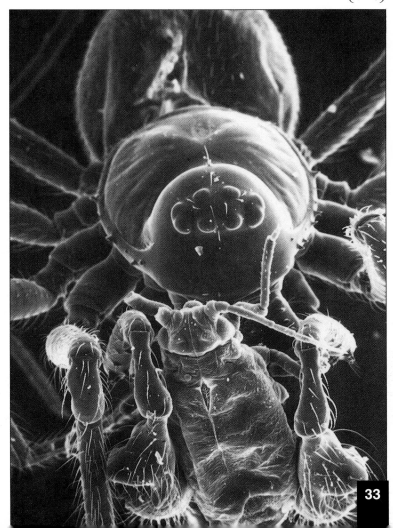

DID YOU KNOW?

Some spiders that live in holes in the ground and under logs in the forests of South America, Asia, and Africa are big enough to eat birds. They have apple-size bodies and legs as long as pencils. These spiders also eat small mammals and insects.

▶ **A spider uses its strong jaws to bite its prey and kill it, sometimes with poison. Then it sucks out the insides of its victim.**

CREEPY CRAWLIES

If you lift a stone or a piece of rotting wood in a garden, park, or field, you may see small creatures running away from the light to hide in dark, damp places. These creatures may include sow bugs, millipedes, and centipedes. They have no wings, their bodies have many linked sections, and they have many jointed legs. These little creepy crawlies are often called bugs, though they are not true insects.

DID YOU KNOW?

Some types of millipedes protect themselves with clouds of poisonous gas. When attacked by predators, such as an army of ants, they release deadly hydrogen cyanide from vents along their bodies. Then they crawl away, leaving the gas behind them.

Rolled-up sow bug

Head of sow bug
(x 60)

◄ **Bendy bodies.** Sow bugs, which are also called wood lice, pill bugs, or slaters, are the only land-living relatives of crabs, lobsters, and shrimps. Their bodies are covered with hard gray plates that are linked like armor. A sow bug can roll itself into a tight ball when in danger. Sow bugs hide in damp places and have to keep their bodies moist. If they dry out, they die. Sow bugs often come out at night to feed on leaves and wood, dead insects, and ripe fruit.

► **A millipede uses its two antennae and the fine hairs on its head to find food.**

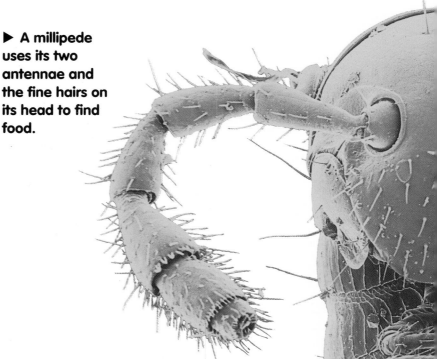

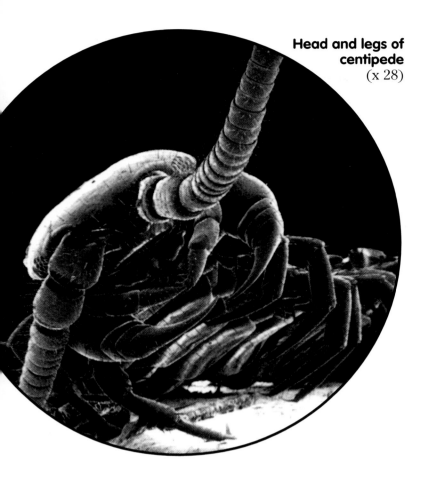

Head and legs of centipede
(x 28)

◄ Loads of legs. Centipedes have a body made up of many sections, with a pair of legs on each. They rest by day and come out from their hiding places at night to feed. Centipedes eat worms, insects, and spiders, catching them with their strong jaws. They bite them and inject a poison that paralyzes the prey. The word *centipede* means "a hundred legs," but some kinds have as few as 34 legs, while others have more than 300.

Millipedes are easy to tell apart from centipedes. For one thing, they have two pairs of legs on each section of their body instead of one. They move slowly, feeding on soft rotting plants and leaves. Millipedes can also be pests, attacking farm crops such as sugar beets.

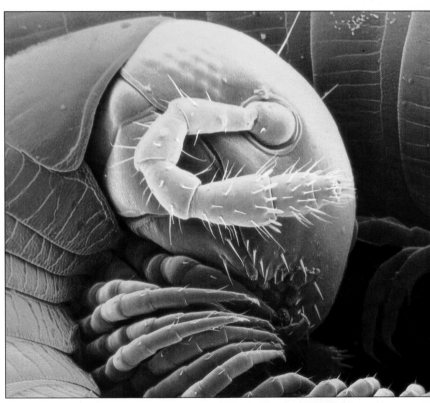

Curled-up millipede
(x 50)

Head of millipede
(x 60)

► This young pill millipede has curled itself into a tight ball in self-defense. When millipedes first hatch, they have only three pairs of legs. More legs are added as the body grows more sections.

IN TROPICAL COUNTRIES THERE ARE CENTIPEDES THAT ARE AS LONG AS THIS PAGE. THEIR POISON CAN KILL BIRDS.

GUESS WHAT?

Read the clues, then try to guess what these images are. You'll find the answers at the bottom of the page.

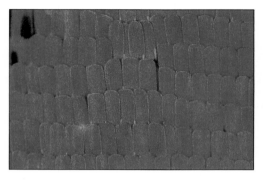

1. Blue slate roof? These "tiles" have a habit of flying off.

2. Expert etching? This work of art will soon be split into pieces by its young owner.

3. Sharp shears? You just might see a pair of these in your garden shed, but not among the tools.

6. Beautiful brooch? This would have a pin in it only if it were unlucky enough to find its way into a museum display case.

4. Crash landing? The creature that lives in this tiny capsule will not be earthbound for long.

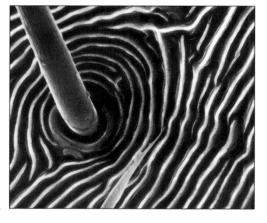

5. Swirls and whirls? The creature that owns this has spinning down to a fine art.

7. Monster's paw? One of nature's sweetest gifts is inside the structure gripping this tree trunk.

8. Alien attack? Some farmers live in dread of an invasion of these.

1. Wing scales of butterfly (x 140) 2. Surface detail of butterfly's eggs (x 550) 3. Pincerlike tail part of earwig (x 10) 4. Butterfly egg (x 40) 5. Spider skin (x 600) 6. Harlequin beetle 7. Natural honeycomb

GLOSSARY

Abdomen — the lower part of the body of an insect or a spider. It contains the parts needed to digest food and to reproduce.

Antennae — long, flexible feelers that help insects find out what is going on around them. Insects use their antennae mainly for smell and touch.

Arachnids — the group of animals that includes spiders, scorpions, mites, and ticks. Creatures in this group always have eight legs and are not considered insects.

Caterpillars — the wormlike larvae of butterflies or moths.

Chitin — the hard material that makes up the outer casing of an insect's body. Some insects' wings are also made of chitin.

Chrysalis — a stage in the development of some insects when a protective covering is formed around the young insect. Some caterpillars, grubs, or maggots stay in their chrysalises only during winter. Others may stay there for years.

Compound eye — a complex eye made up of hundreds or thousands of tiny six-sided cells packed closely together. Each cell acts like an eye and collects slightly different information, which the brain combines into one picture.

Cornicles — two short tubes on the backs of some aphids. These tubes produce a waxy liquid that helps the aphid to escape from the jaws of its predators.

Facet — one of the many surfaces that make up an insect's compound eye. The facet is a lens that focuses light down a rod made up of layers of light-detecting cells. The insect's brain combines the information from the different rods all over the eye and produces a single picture.

Mandibles — the strong, sharp jaws of some insects that allow them to hold and bite food.

Metamorphosis — one of a series of changes that many insects go through before they become adults. The changes usually happen in three or four stages.

Millipedes — creatures whose bodies are made up of many segments, usually with two pairs of legs on each section. Millipedes are similar to centipedes, which have only one pair of legs on each section.

Molting — the shedding of an insect's hard outside skin so that the insect can grow larger.

Nectar — a sugary liquid made by some plants. Some birds, bats, and many insects feed on nectar.

Parasite — a creature that lives on or in another plant or animal, feeding on it while it is still alive. Parasites can cause illness in animals and completely destroy crops.

Pollen — a fine powder produced by flowers. Bees use it to make honey. They collect the pollen in special "baskets" on their legs and carry it back to their hive.

Proboscis — a long mouth tube, or hollow tongue, that an insect uses for sucking up its food.

Spinnerets — tubes at the end of a spider's body that produce the silken thread for the spider's web. Very fine threads come out of the many openings in each spinneret and join together to make one thread.

Spiracles — small holes in an insect's thorax (middle) and abdomen through which it breathes.

Thorax — the middle section of an insect's body. All six of its legs, plus its wings (if it has any), are attached to its thorax.

Wing scales — broad, flattened hairs, overlapping like roof tiles, that make up the wings of butterflies and moths and some other insects.

INDEX

The authors and publishers would like to thank Andrew Syred of Microscopix, Liz Hirst at the National Institute of Medical Research, and Steve Gorton for their assistance in the preparation of this book, as well as the other photographers and organizations listed below for their kind permission to reproduce the following photographs:

Dr. Tony Brain: 5 bottom right, 25 center, right of center, and bottom right, 27 bottom right, 28 bottom left, 29 top, 30 bottom, 31 right of center, 34 bottom left

David Burder: 32 bottom

Bruce Coleman: 21 bottom; **Norman Tomalin**: 25 top

Steve Gschmeisner: 6-7 center, 7 left, 12 right, 16 center and right, 17 top left and left of center, 33 bottom right

Liz Hirst/NIMR: 26-27 bottom, 27 center

Natural History Museum, London: 3 bottom left, 8 right of center, 9 bottom left, 13 left of center, 14-15 bottom, 15 bottom right, 20 right, 21 right of center, 23 bottom left, 28 center and right of center, 29 bottom, 36 right of center

Nature Photographers/Brinsley Burbidge: 11 top right; **Geoff du Feu**: 18 top left; **Paul Sterry**: 8 top left

NHPA/Anthony Bannister: 12 left; **George Bernard**: 36 left of center; **Andy Callow**: 34 left of center; **James Carmichael**: 5 center, 17 bottom; **Stephen Dalton**: 26 top, 28 top, 36 bottom right; **Peter Johnson**: 31 left of center

Rothamsted Experimental Station: 35 top left

Science Photo Library/Dr. Brad Amos: 23 right of center; **Biophoto Associates**: 34-35 bottom; **Dr. Tony Brain**: 30 top, 31 bottom left; **Dr. Jeremy Burgess**: 3 left of center, 5 bottom left, 10 top right and bottom right, 11 left and bottom right, 13 bottom right, 14 top left, left of center, and bottom left, 15 top right, 16 left, 17 top right, 19 top left, 20 left, 21 top left, 22 left and right, 23 top left, 24 top, center, and bottom, 35 bottom right; **Darwin Dale**: 10 bottom left; **Judy Davidson**: 7 bottom right; **Catherine Ellis/Dept. of Zoology, Hull University** : 7 top; **Stevie Grand**: 4 bottom left; **Adam Hart-Davis**: 32 top left; **Manfred Kage**: 3 right, 13 bottom left; **J. C. Revy** : 36 top right; **David Scharf**: 1, 13 top right, 14 right, 18-19 bottom, 19 top right, 26 bottom left, 27 top right, 32-33 top, 33 center and top right, 36 bottom left; **Jeremy Trew**: 4 top left

Andrew Syred/Microscopix: 4 top right, right of center, bottom right, and below center, 6 left of center, bottom left, and below center, 8 left of center and center, 9 top and bottom right, 23 above center and bottom right, 31 top right, 36 top left, above center, and center

ILLUSTRATORS:

Paul Richardson 6
All other illustrations by Jane Gedye